I AM WATER

MEG SPECKSGOOR

An imprint of Enslow Publishing

WEST 44 BOOKS™

Please visit our website, www.west44books.com.
For a free color catalog of all our high-quality books,
call toll free 1-800-542-2595 or fax 1-877-542-2596.

Cataloging-in-Publication Data

Names: Specksgoor, Meg.
Title: I am water / Meg Specksgoor.
Description: New York : West 44, 2020. | Series: West 44 YA verse
Identifiers: ISBN 9781538382790 (pbk.) | ISBN 9781538382806
  (library bound) | ISBN 9781538383407 (ebook)
Subjects: LCSH: Children's poetry, American. | Children's poetry,
  English. | English poetry.
Classification: LCC PS586.3 S643 2020 | DDC 811'.60809282--dc23

First Edition

Published in 2020 by
Enslow Publishing LLC
101 West 23rd Street, Suite #240
New York, NY 10011

Copyright © 2020 Enslow Publishing LLC

Editor: Caitie McAneney
Designer: Seth Hughes

Printed in the United States of America

CPSIA compliance information: Batch #CS18W44: For further information contact
Enslow Publishing LLC, New York, New York at 1-800-542-2595.

The Thing About Rivers

They have
a way
of f l o w i n g
through you
when
you've worked
on one
long enough.

Guide a river
for
a few years
and
it ends up
guiding
you.

The Way It Moves

People climb
in my boat
every day.
I introduce myself—
Hi, I'm Hannah.
They are eager-eyed.
Wearing
wet suits.
Nervous
excitement.
They understand
the thrill
in
the moment.
But
they don't
understand
the way
the water
winds its way
into
my veins.
Creating channels
that feed
into
my heart
like
a stream.

My Guests

I guide families
with children
who watch
each drop
and bend
with a
mix
of
fear
and
joy.

Students
from
the inner city
whose feet are
confident
on concrete,
but
unsure
in
moving
water.

Men and women
on dates or
anniversaries.
Going well
or poorly.

Boy Scouts
looking
to prove
their
grit.
Earn
their
merit badges.

And everyone
in
between.

The water
does not
judge.
Only
punishes
the ones
who
don't
respect
it.

September

The man
in the
front of
my raft
is a
scoutmaster.
Easily
twice
my age.

The water
silvers
the hair
under his
wide
hat.

I turn
the bow
to steer
toward
river left.
My hands
firmly grip
my
guide stick.
He corrects me
with
a stroke on
the right.

Like he's
been doing
for an hour.
Typical.

"Stop steering
my boat,"
I half
command,
half
plead.
"That's
my job."

"I've been
canoeing
since
before you
were born.
So
I think
I know
what I'm
doing,"
he replies.
Gives
a smug
laugh.

"Great,
you know
the person
in the back
steers,"

I say.
I match
his snark.

He darts me
a quick look.
Like
who do you
think you are?
The way only
middle-aged men
talking to
high school girls
know how.

He is
about
to say
something
more. But
I yell
for
everyone
to
paddle
forward.

We're
coming up to
the first of
three
Class III
rapids.
All in a row.
I'm going

to need
their cooperation
to keep
the boat straight.

His wife and
two sons
stroke for me.
Right on cue.
But
the father
slips in
a strong
back paddle
just before
a boulder.
It throws off
my control.

The bow
crashes
into the rock.
Water explodes.
His wife
is spilled
overboard.

The rapid
flushes her
through
two drops.
Kicking
and
crying.
Forgetting

8

every
rule
from the safety talk.
Remain calm.
Let the water
take you.

I finally
get her
back
into the boat.
Her face is as
white as
the top
of a
wave.

Her eyes
as big as
the holes
she
just
avoided.

The husband
rages
on
about my
lack of skill.
We
arrive
onshore
tired
and
defeated.

It is
always
men
who try
to run
a
river
for
me.

The Thing About High School

It isn't
much different
sometimes.
Just a big,
unforgiving
river.

Full of boys
who will
grow up to be
silvery men.
Wearing
wide hats.
Thinking
their strokes are
always right.

Girls like
shiny pools with
bubbly laughs.

Boys smooth as
wave trains.
Leading
straight to whirlpools
you'll never survive.

Then there's
the rest of us.

The backwash.
We are
the eddies.
The edges
of river
outside
the mainstream.
We run
against
the natural
flow of things.

That's where
the flotsam
meets
and curdles.

That's where
the safety is.
But
also
where you
can get stuck.

Once in an eddy,
it can be
pretty difficult
to turn yourself
back into the current.

Once you
become an eddy,
you never run
with the fast
crowd again.

They blow
by you.
In a show of
spray
and sun gleam.
Rushing
unstoppably.
And you
can't
catch
up.

That's where
Sam and I
are.

Sam, the Arsonist

Sam has hair
that,
if it were
a temperature
instead of
a color,
would be
boiling.
Which fits
with his love
of fire.

He keeps a
purple lighter
in his
pocket.
He's always
playing
with it,
even though
he doesn't
smoke.

"Anxiety,"
he says.
  The flame
    puts him in
       a calming trance.
         He's best known
           in town

for burning down
his neighbor's
shed.
Stray
homemade firework
one
Independence Day.
His parents
were
away.

I'm not sure
who started it.
But, since then,
folks here
call him
"Arsonist Sam."
Or just
"Arsam"
for short.

It may be
a small dairy
and lumber town.
No
art gallery
or theater in sight.
But I guess
we're not
completely
without
creativity.
I was
the first
to see

the
backyard blaze.
I ran,
panting.
Sam
was
staring
at the colors
in awe.

"Are you crazy?"
I screamed.

That broke
whatever
red-orange
spell
had
bewitched
his mind.

He
looked at me
slowly.
A
fire of
his own
glowed
within
his eyes.

It had been
an accident,
sure.

But he
wasn't
terrified.

He almost
seemed
excited
about the
consequence.

"Yeah,
probably,"
he said.
"But
not as
crazy
as
my parents
will
be."

The fire
in his eyes
blazed.

"At least now
they'll have
to notice me."

I grabbed
the hose.
Sprayed
the flames
licking
the side of

the shed.
Like waves
lapping
the side of
my boat.

He made
no move
to help.

Then,
once the only
colors
left on
the roof
were
black soot
and
white ash,
I turned the hose
on Sam.

And soaked
every
last
inch
of him.

"You have
so much
heat
inside you,
you're going to
burn up
one day if

you're not
careful."

For a second
he looked like
he might kill me
then and there.
But the anger
in his face
melted to
a sly
sort of
respect.

"What did you say
your name was?"

That's when
a friendship
was born
out of the balance
of a natural truth:
Water
puts out fire.

Water Dream #1

The night
before
the first day
of junior year,
I have a
water dream.

They come
and go.
Usually
to tell me
something
important.

The lens of
my sight is
aqua and
cloudy.
Just above
the river bottom.

The fish are
streamlining
through the current.
But then
they start to
act strange.
Squirming
and darting.

Out of
nowhere,
I drift
straight into
a deposit
of dirt
and
a fallen tree.

There's
no way
around or
under it.
I'm
tangled up
in the roots.
I go
deeper
and deeper
into
the twisted mess
of branches
and weeds
the more
I struggle.

I wake up
cold
and
clammy.

Something
is
coming.

An Entrance

We've
only gotten
through
first period
when Sam
finds me
in the
hallway.

He reaches
into his
coat pocket.
I can tell
he's fiddling
with the lighter,
which he could
get suspended
for carrying.

His eyes are
flickering
like a
match.

"Have you
seen the
new kid?"

He doesn't
have to
explain
much further.
Because
in a minute,
I see
him.
And know
instantly
that
this
is who
everyone
is
whispering
about.

An Impression

First of all,
he doesn't
walk.
He strides.

Dark curls fall
across his forehead
with grace.
As much
as the
sheer purple scarf
with glittering
silver moons
beaming from
shoulder to
shoulder.

He wears a
black turtleneck,
straight cut jeans,
and heeled boots.
I swear
you'd be able
to hear them
from
the other end
of the hallway.
Even if
the other students
hadn't gone

suddenly
mute.
A perfectly
arched
eyebrow
curves
like
a smirk.
Into
a dainty
metal hoop.

Beneath,
eyes greener
than
grass
catch mine
for
an instant.
And
he
passes
by.

One thing
is
for sure.
Whoever
he is,
he's
not
from
here.

Detailed Reports

Rumors
circulate
faster
than blood
in this school.
So by
fifth period,
I've had
an earful.

He
moved here
from
the city
a week
ago.

His parents
went
to California
for business.
So he
hauled himself
six hours
to his aunt's house.
For his last year
of high school.
Rather than adjust
to the West Coast
as a senior.

He doesn't
eat
lunch.
Just handfuls
of nuts
and
locker snacks.

While
everyone else
chows down in
the cafeteria,
he sits under
a tree in
the schoolyard.
Plucking
a **mandolin**.
A mandolin,
of all things.

The science teacher
made a joke about
his outfit.
Said a gypsy
had come to town.
The new kid asked
what the teacher's
sign was.
His **sign**.

When told
Aries,
he hmm'ed
and said,
"I thought so."

*His
name
is
Ezra.*

The Best Class of the Day

I have
the table
farthest
from
the door
all to
myself
in art class.
Just the way
I like it.

Then,
I hear
the stool
next to me
squeak
as it is
scooched
across the floor.

I turn
to see
a cascade of
dark curls.
The boy
adjusts
his
purple
scarf.

Water Dream #2

I'm fishing
in the pond
behind
my grandfather's
cabin.

Everyone
told me
the stock had
run dry.
But I've
never much
listened
to everyone.

I get a bite.

It's the
biggest fish
I've seen in
my life.
Scales
shining in
colors
I didn't know
were possible.

Rainbows
upon rainbows
of shades

not yet
discovered.

The fish
doesn't
thrash
or
struggle.
Just
eyes me
coolly.
Knowingly.
Before
pulling
me
in.

Renny and the Woodshop Stool

That week I drag
a stool
to the doorway of
my brother Renny's room.
The special stool
he made for me
in the woodshop where
he works.

Sometime within
the last year, this
became my signal for
can we talk?

He looks up.
Brown hair, messy
as the bed he sits on,
winding down his face.
It sits beneath
the ball cap
I swear he's done
everything but shower in
since he was eight.

That's Renny:
ball caps and drab flannel.
Living proof of
the things in this town
that will never change.

He gives me
a quick nod,
flipping his hair
toward
the foot of the bed.
His returned signal.
I drag
the stool in.

Just as I'm
about to spill,
his cell phone rings.
It's Veronica,
the cosmetology queen.
Miss Americana herself.

Blonde hair long as
the sighs she brings out
of my lovesick brother.
Bright blue eyelids.
Plum lipstick.
Rouge to fake
a shy blush.

They were
high school sweethearts.
He,
the captain of
the baseball team.
She,
a cheerleader.
Bottom of the pyramid though.
Until she became
Renny's girl.

Before
Renny graduated,
he had scouts
from colleges
throughout the state
itching
to give him
a jersey.

It shocked us
when he turned
every last one
down.
Asked
the local carpenter
for a job.

He was a natural,
of course,
whether
swinging wood
or crafting it.
But Veronica
hasn't seen it
that way.
She's glad
he's still in town
for her last year of school.
But she was hoping
to be the kind of
senior girl who dates
a college boy.
A college jock,
no less.

Her family
got some money
from a dead, rich
great-aunt
in some big city.
So she started
wearing makeup
and talking big
to match
the glamour
of how
her life would
soon be.

University.
Theater.
A few minor
acting gigs
to start off small.
Suddenly sure
this was all
within her reach.

Loving my brother
until she moved on
to higher society.
It became her
first role,
I fear.
But it'd kill him
if I said it.
And in this case,
I want so badly
to be wrong.

They make
a Friday night
date.
He ruffles
his scraggly hair
in absentminded
excitement.
Hangs up.

He adjusts his
ball cap.
Like he does
whenever
he switches
from giddy
to serious.

"So, Hannah," he says.
"Spill."

"Well,
I'm not sure
what to say
really,"
I start.
"There's
this
new kid
at
school."

I Spill Again

In class,
we are learning
conceptual art.
Art that is art
because of the thought
and not the look.
Not because
we're so
high-minded,
though.

It's because
Mrs. Bently
got tired of
smashing inappropriate
clay sculptures
students tried
to convince her
were vases
for their
mothers.

She
got tired of
setting up the same
overdone
bowl of pears
or table of
deer skulls
for still-life
paintings.

Most of all,
I think,
she got tired of
adding her own money to
the budget for canvas
and other supplies.

The school has cut
a lot of funding.
And concept is
cheaper than oil paint.
Just found materials
and brainpower.

I am painting
detailed, unreal
sea creatures
in watercolors.
Mixing paint
with water
I took from the river.
My river.

Any muck or grit
adds texture.
Context.
Instead of
getting in the way.

I don't plan
what the creatures
will look like.
Just let each drop of river
show me what it has seen.
What it imagines.

Ezra is
putting together
photographs he
took with
a 35-millimeter
film camera.

They all look
overexposed
or underexposed.
Mostly blurs
of light
and
fuzzy figures.
Or dark spaces.
You can
barely make anything out.
Except for
hazy objects.

They dangle,
mobile-like.
Attached
by wires.
The way a
diagram of
the planets would.

Astrology symbols
are drawn over each.
They have to do with
the time of year,
the people he was with,
and the feeling
it gave him.

He says
he makes
the photos
look
that way
on purpose.
Because that is
how his
memory is.
Hazy.
Fuzzy.
Barely
understandable
sometimes.

I wonder
who
these people are,
these bursts
of light
and smudges
of color.

For a minute,
I'm a little
jealous.

They hang
grandly.
Like stars.
Forever frozen
inside
a universe
he made
just for them.

For a minute,
I wish I
could be
suspended
there
in the
orbit
of his
thoughts.

A
watery
green–blue
cloud.

I wonder
what his
impression
of me
would
look
like.

There's a photo
he claims
is a self-portrait.
It looks like a night sky
ripping open with
streaks of
blinding white light.

"It's not colorful enough
to be you,"
I say.

His lips curve into
a sly grin.
"White light contains
all the colors,"
he says.

Above his self-portrait
is an arrow with
a line through it.

"What's that?" I ask.

"Sagittarius." He winks
like a star twinkling.

"I'm a Capricorn
by birth," he says.
"But the only truth
to that
is its Earth sign.
Every other bit
of my chart
is Sag.
Fire.
You
are water,"
he says.
"But I
can't decide
which
symbol."

"I'm
a Pisces."

His lips
purse.
His perfect
brows
tense.
"Hmm.
Interesting."

"What?" I ask.

"Well,
the stars
seem to think
we'd be
very
attracted
to each other.
But
not
compatible
at
all."

I'm so
taken aback.
Delighted
and put out
all at once.
I bump into
my jar
and
the river
comes
pouring
out.

It smears
my latest
creature
until I can't
recognize it.
So it looks
exactly like
it belongs in
one of
the photos
in his
mobile.

"There,"
he says.
"Now
it's in
my
memory."

Coffee Shop Fridays

Renny
agrees
to drive
Sam and me
to the
coffee shop
before his date.
We don't have
our licenses
yet.

Every
Friday,
we split
a milkshake.
We take turns
picking
the flavor.

Tonight,
Sam picks
Fireball.

I joke that
he just
likes it
for the
name.

Afterward,
we walk
to the
quarry.
To our
secret
spot.

The Quarry, Waxing Crescent, Harvest Moon

I collect
the wood
and Sam
builds the fire.
That's the deal.
As always.
We laugh
and tease
and gossip
for an hour.
Smiles
crackling
like
the
flames.

Eventually,
a call
from Renny
tells us
it's time
to put out
the blaze.

We walk back
to the open road.
The smell of
wood smoke
and
good secrets
sticking
to
our
clothes.

Unexpected Growth

Ezra asked
the science teacher
if he could
take over
the rundown
greenhouse
behind the
gymnasium.

"It looked like
an overgrown
cemetery.
Or a
ghost town
of abandoned
dirt and weeds,"
he said.
"I'm taking
care of it
after school.
I've
always been
good
at gardening.
Planting it
using the
lunar
calendar.

Come next year
there'll be
so many flowers
and herbs.
Natives
and exotics.
This town
will have
never seen
anything like it.
They don't
even know
the variety
of life
that can grow
in this soil."

I smile at this.
At how quickly
a foreign plant
can take root
here.

At how
naturally
Ezra adapts
to my home.
Even if
he is
the most
diverse life
to ever attempt
growth
in this soil.

A Clash

At lunch,
I tell Ezra
to hang up
the
mandolin
and sit
with
Sam and me.

He's wearing
bronze
eyeliner.
A forest green
pullover
made of
wool.
Burgundy
corduroys.

He beams and
tells stories of
living in the city.
Of equinox
parties
and of
new
moon
gatherings.
I take it
all in,

enjoying it
like high water
in the spring.
When the
snowmelt
and rain
turn the river
into a rush
of chocolate
milk-colored
swells and surfs.
And the current is
so fast
you can
barely
stop a boat.

Sam is
quiet.
Not
a polite
quiet.

I glance
under the table
and catch him
flicking
his lighter.
On and off.
On
and
off.

A Falling-Out

Sam and I split
a Panda Paws
milkshake.
My choice.
Sam is
talking about
a girl in
World History
who didn't know
we fought
the British
for independence.

He's just getting
to the punchline
when
I break my gaze.
Ezra
walks by
the window
in a flowing
cream tunic.
Curls bouncing
lightly
as he steps.

The drink catches
in my throat
and I choke.

Suddenly
it's like bellows
have roared
the coals
in Sam's
amber eyes.
"Don't tell me
you actually
like that guy,"
he scoffs.

"So what if I do?"
I ask.
"And I'm not
saying I do."

"He's just
so vain
and arrogant,"
Sam says.
"And he always
has to
stand out."

"You're just
jealous
that he does it
so easily,"
I say back.
Which was
a mistake. Because
Sam lurches
out of his chair
and walks out the door.

Slamming it
behind him.
I don't think
I've ever seen
his eyes in
such
a heat.

I look down at
our milkshake.
There's still
half
of it
left.

The Quarry, Hunter's Moon

I'm feeling
pretty crummy.
But I still have
another hour
before Renny
will pull up
in his pickup truck.
I decide
to go down to
our secret spot
anyway.

Tonight is
a full moon.
And she's
pulling on me
like she pulls
on every other
body of water.

I can't help it.
When I get to
the river's edge,
I strip off my jacket
and jeans.
I wade in.
Just enough for
the reflected moonbeams
to drift into me.

Soak into my skin.
It's freezing,
but
the cold numbs
the fire
Sam left
behind.

"Ehemm."
A throat clears
from somewhere
on the other side
of the bushes.

"I knew you
were a
shapeshifter
the first time
I met you.
A water creature
who has to return
every so often
to keep
the spell going.
Don't try
to deny it."

In the pale light,
I can just see
a flowing
cream tunic
and curls.

Ezra.

"Don't worry.
I'll look away
while you
slip your
land legs
back on
and
hide
your gills."

I redress,
half
embarrassed,
half
curious.

He is sitting
on the rocks,
burning
a small pile
of sage.
Eyes closed.

I come
close enough
to see
that his lashes
are thick
and black.
Dusted
ever so slightly
with
stray specks
of
glitter.

"I do this
on every
full moon,"
he says.
"I cleanse
myself
and my
surroundings.
Send up
prayers
to the
sacred."

"What do you
pray for?"
I ask.

He inches forward
as if to tell me
a great
and terrible
secret.
"For fish
to become
beautiful women
and men
to become
fairies.
And for
every
transformation
once
thought of
as impossible."

"Really?"
I say,
sliding
closer.
I whisper,
"Any
luck?"

"On
at least
one account."

He pulls
a fleece-lined
jacket
from the rocks
he was
sitting on and
wraps it
tight
around
my shivering
shoulders.

He looks over
at my
dripping,
cold feet.
"You
no longer
have fins."

And then
I'm
leaning into
those
glitter-speckled
eyelashes
until
they flood
my vision
like
shooting stars.
His curls
brush against
my forehead
and
his lips
are
on mine.

Soft.
Fluid.
Like
moonlight
on
water.

Water Dream #3

My legs
meld
together
and sprout
scales.

I touch the water and
it shimmers out
from my fingertips.
Beautiful
silver ripples.
The glittering curves
are like crescent moons
or
Ezra's eyes.

I can breathe
underwater
all the way to
the base of a
towering waterfall.

I dive below and
surface behind it.
Wild vines
and flowers
the size of my face
weave a
tropical jungle.

I crawl onto
a heap of moss
and ferns.
The ground
is so warm
beneath me.

Then,
I hear his voice.
His tinkling voice,
say,
"Hannah, I knew
you were a
shapeshifter."

I
am
water.
And
he
is
earth.

Hidden

On the way into school
the next day, I
pass Ezra on the sidewalk.
His smile is all
flirt and glimmer.
But he flinches when
I grab his hand.
Peers over his shoulder.
Eyes flitting nervously,
to see if anyone behind us
is watching.
He says,
"Best not to let anyone know.
You agree?"

"But why?" I ask.

"Just trust me, okay?
It wouldn't be good for us
if certain people found out."

I'm about to protest, but
he squeezes my fingers
to assure me.

Then he lets them slip.
Putting the doubts in my mind
at ease.

"Well, alright then," I say.

January

He says
I water
the grass
inside
his head.
That
whenever
I'm near,
his mind
runs
barefoot.

March

He leaves me
bits of treasures
from his
greenhouse
in my locker.

Pansies
to show
he's thinking
of me.

White clover
to ask me
to think
of him.

Jasmine,
for love.

I bring home
the clippings
and put them
in a mug
in my room.

I will feed them
water
to sustain
them.

I will feed him
water
to sustain
him.

Bo, Incident #1

Ezra has been sitting
with us in the lunchroom
regularly for months now.

Sam didn't like it at first.
But he cooled off.
After I apologized for
what I said at the coffee shop.

Something new has
started to happen
over the last few weeks.
Girls I've never
talked to before
are sitting with us, too.
Girls who aren't eddies.
Girls who flow
with the mainstream.
Girls like Victoria.

They question Ezra
endlessly.
About fashion.
And the city.
And the secrets of the stars.
They ask to see
his tarot cards.
Ask for him to read
their palms.
Ask for stories about

what the moon
tells him.
Sometimes
I can't help but
feel left out.
Feel like
I am a riptide.
Tugging on him
to join me
in the sea.
While
five senior girls
stand on shore,
in sunhats and shades
and polka dot bikinis,
and wave him
back in.

But then
he catches
my glance
and smiles.
Ever so slightly.
Too sly for
the rest of
the table to notice.

It's then that I picture
myself as salt water.
The kind that gives itself
with fondness
to his skin.

Reminding him of the ocean
long after he has left it.

A secret intimacy.
Out of the corner
of my eye,
I see Bo
and his posse
at a table
not far from us.

Spiked hair.
Ripped jeans.
Studded belt.
Muscle tank.
Bo wouldn't be
caught dead
taking fashion advice
from anyone.
Let alone
a boy with
glittered eyes
and a moon scarf.

He is snickering and
elbowing Derek.
Gesturing toward
our table.
Mouthing the word
"fag."

The water boils
inside me.
I make note
to prepare
a shipwreck
if I need to.

Looking back
at Ezra,
I decide,
yes.
I can be
salt water.

Salt water
to clean
stinging
wounds.

Salt water
to cradle
his body.
Lifting it
to the surface
with
invisible
hands.
Keeping
his head
above
water.

Bo, Incident #2

Ezra is showing me
the sprouts
in his greenhouse.
Life
breaking ground
in emerald
and olive
and gold.
A boy
walking by
outside
shouts,
"Homo!"
as he races
by the door.

I recognize
Bo's
deep,
rocky
voice.

Ezra ignores him.
The green
of his eyes
dulls to
a gray hazel.
He looks toward
the now-empty
doorway.

Then gazes at
the ground
in silence.

After a minute he says,
"Do you know why
people don't want weeds?"

I don't see
where he's going
with this.

"Because they kill
what someone is
trying to plant.

But a weed is
just something
unwanted.
What is and isn't
a weed
depends on
what plants
someone wants.

A dandelion
is considered
a pest. But
not to someone who
makes wine from
the petals.
Some of the most
beautiful flowers
are wild and would
take over

a garden if someone
would let them.
Most plants people
consider weeds are more
natural to the area than
the ones they import.
Most have stronger roots. And
many make good homes
for small animals.
Animals also considered pests."

"You're not a weed,"
I say.
"And you're not unwanted."

"Maybe not by you.
But I'm definitely not
the kind of thing
this town would like to see grow.
Though,
somewhere else,
like back in the city,
I'd be left alone.
Maybe even helped.

Did you know
plants
can protect
themselves?"
he asks.

I shake my head.
I wait for him to continue.

"Nature is full of

interesting species.
Mimosa plants
actually
curl away
from human hands.
They know touch
can be damaging.
So
they don't
let themselves
be touched."

"You're not
a coward,"
I say.
"Sometimes
protecting yourself
is necessary."

He continues.
"Nightshade
can kill a man."

"You're not
violent like that,"
I say.

"Poison ivy
grows on land
that has been
torn
and ruined.
To keep people
from doing
any more harm.

Until the plants
regrow.
A defender."

"That sounds
more like you,"
I say.
"A defender.
Ivy breaks through
cement and brick.
Bur oaks are
fireproof."

He smiles
gratefully
as I continue.

"Strong.
The earth
is strong.
Like you.
Fireproof.
Which is good
because
Bo is
a fire sign."

He looks me
straight in
the eye
and
I reach out
with
fingertips
to his

cheek.

He doesn't
curl away
like a
mimosa
would.
Instead,
the green
relights
in
his
eyes.

Makeshift Horoscope for Today

On my desk
later that day.
A handwritten
horoscope.

Pisces:
Tonight is
a favorable time
for romance.

The stars
shine down on
a relationship with
a devilishly
handsome partner.
(Meet me
at the river,
10:00 pm.)

A Reveal

I tell Sam
I have plans after
our weekly milkshake.
He eyes
my midnight blue
cotton dress
and lace tights
like he knows
something is up.
I almost always
wear baggy jeans and
an earth-toned zip-up.

He braces to
ask a million questions.
But I switch the subject
to chemistry,
the one class he
now loves.
Mr. Ralph taught them to make
molten iron and fires that
can't be put out with water.
Questioning dodged.

After our milkshake,
I walk down to
Sam's and my spot.
But Samless,
to meet
Ezra.

Guilt
wells up inside
like a spring.
But Sam
wouldn't understand.
And I get why
Ezra doesn't want
to go somewhere
like a movie theater,
where he might
run into any
of the guys
from school.

The Quarry, Waxing Gibbous, Egg Moon

He's there waiting
with
a potted
philodendron.
A gift.
But
he looks
nervous.
Like he needs
to tell
a secret and
he doesn't
know
if he can.

"What's on
your mind?"
I ask.

"I know
what people
are saying
about me,
but
I'm not
gay. And
I'm not
bisexual.
I'm
gender fluid."

He talks fast
as he
explains to me
what it means to be
both a man
and a woman.
At one point
he seems to be
at a loss for words.
Until
he looks up to see
the moon.

He continues,
"It's kind of like
the moon
is the feminine me
and the sun
is the masculine me
everyone expects
me to be.

The moon is always there,
but, during the day,
the sun mostly
overpowers her.

Sometimes,
if you look
closely though,
you can see her.
Faintly.
But it is only when
she is left alone
and the sun sleeps

that she can give off
her full light.

Other times,
one
eclipses
the other
and
I can't find
a piece of
myself.
And
everything
goes
dark.

Those times
are hard."

I can tell
he's
troubled by
my quietness.
He probably thinks
I'm
freaked out
by his truth.
But
it's entirely
the opposite.

A dam opens up
inside my chest.
All the things that have been
caught in the backwash

between my head
and my throat
flood my mind.

Once
you are told
how water works,
you understand
things you have
experienced
on a river.

Once
I was told
how gender works,
as Ezra went on
in detail about
social constructs and
being outside
the binary,
I understood
things I had
experienced
in life.

I understood
the slumber parties
I never wanted to attend.

I understood
my confused sadness
at my parents'
disapproval when
I cut my own hair with
a bowl and scissors.

Age eight. And
ran off to the creek with
the boys next door.

I understood
my outer pride
every time
someone praised me
for being a strong girl in
a man's job.
But also
my inner need
sometimes
to pretend
I am
just
another
boy
on
the
river.

The river.
Nature
is full of
species that
have no gender.
Or
change gender.
Or
break the norm of
what gender
should mean.

Fluid.

Like
a river.
Like
water.

I smile
and
a single tear
wanders
down my
cheek.

I nod.
"I'm
not sure.
But
I think,
maybe,
me
too."

His face is
a mix of
relief,
surprise,
and
excitement.

"Can we
try something?"
he asks.

An Evolution

It's 11:00 on
a Friday night.
Teenagers,
classmates,
hang out in front of
the box office.
On street corners.
Outside the coffee shop.
Ezra and I
stroll
hand in hand
down
Main Street.
I in his
black jeans
and button-up shirt.
He in my
midnight blue
cotton dress
and lace tights.
Heads start
to turn.
And whispers turn
to jeers.
I grasp his hand
tighter in mine.

"You look beautiful,"
I say.

He looks at me.
For the first time
all night,
his eyes are
focused.
Calm.
Steady.

"It's true.
I'm earth and
you're water.
I need
you
in order
to grow."

Then he does
something
that makes
every drop
inside me
surge up like
a towering wave.

He holds my face
in his palms,
as if he were cupping
a very big, fragile seed.
Or a precious drink
of water. And
he kisses me
right on the street.
In the midnight blue light.
In a midnight blue dress.

And I'm
swimming
through the sky.
Swirling and
stroking
endlessly
through the
depth.
And
the only thing
that
brings me
back down
is
the mix
of shock
and anger on
a face in
the crowd.
Lit by
a single
flame
from
a purple
lighter.

A Night of Mixed Dreams

That night I have
two dreams.
An earth dream and
a water dream.

The first.
My room is
filled from
wall to wall with
potted
philodendrons.
They whisper green
to me.
Pulsing.
The green feeds
my imagination's
predawn hunger.
Growing as wild and
huge as the plants
pouring out of
their containers.

The walls drip
moss and nectar.
Sapping and
releasing spores.
Bristling and
breathing.
Ezra is lying

on the bed
next to me.
A mattress
somehow
made of soil.
A garden bed.

A canopy of vines
winds down
his shoulders and
around my waist.

The room
is bright with
magenta and
tangerine.
Forest green and
marigold.
And the plants
take in the colors
like a sort of
photosynthesis.

Ezra says
the philodendrons
don't need much.
He says
he doesn't
need much
either.
But I am
still learning
the things I have
for giving.

He is
bent
around me.
Arms wrapped
around
my middle.
Feet laced
together
into
threaded roots.
Digging
deep
into the
sheets.

The green
behind
our
closed eyes
and in
our stomachs
reassures
us.
It's
enough
to
get
us
through
tomorrow.

A Nightmare

A harbor shimmers
in the speckled
moonlight.
Blue-green and
serene.

There is a thick,
inky blackness.
It dribbles at first,
from somewhere
unknown. But
begins to spew
faster and faster.
Until it's gushing
unstoppably.
Scummy.
Tar-like.
Deathly.
An oil spill.

Then
the whole scene
alights in
a screaming blaze.
Orange and deep red.

The surface
of the water
is burning.

Poise

Red: a single
ball-shaped earring
dangling from
one lobe.

Orange: a pair of
Keds he kicks around in
when his leather boots are
too much.

Yellow: a wool poncho.
Draped like confidence
over strong but
delicate shoulders.

Green: eyes that seem
as hungry
and lively
as the ferns he grows.

Blue: nail polish
he tried before
calling it—
with a wink—
too glitzy
for his humble style.

Purple: a graceful
defiant harmony of
pink and blue,
girl and boy.

This is
the portrait of
Ezra.
As he struts down
a side street
of a
small town
no one in
Paris or
Milan
will ever
hear of.
And not
caring
all the
same.

He wears a chip
on his tooth
from singing in
a punk band.
Just as proudly as
he wears a silk dress
with cutouts.
And that,
in this town,
might be
the most
dangerous
and
exciting
thing
of
all.

Social Deforestation

Neither Victoria, nor
any of her friends,
sit with us at lunch today.

In fact, the whole school
is acting weird.
Like we crossed
some unsaid
line in the sand.
Giving us blank stares
and cold shoulders.

The only thing warm at all—
too hot, in fact—
is Sam's burning stare
when we try
to slide in with him.

I should have told Sam
that we're together.

That I blew him off
for Ezra.

I can tell Ezra thinks it's
because of his outfit today.
That his boldness has
outworn its welcome.
Wearing a dress to school.
To *school*, of all places.
Why would he expect people
to act any differently?

I doubt
it ever
crossed his mind.
For Sam,
perhaps
the kiss
was
more
bold
than
the
fashion.

Bo, Incident #3

Ezra is leaving
the school grounds
at the end of the day
when Bo
reaches him
before I do.

Furious,
he shoves
Ezra by
the shoulders.

"I mean, it was
gross when you
were *just* gay,"
he sneers
through
clenched teeth.

His fists are
balled up.
Tight.
At both sides of
his studded belt.
"When you were
the gay friend.
But what kind of
sick game
are you playing?"

"You think you
can love
a woman
dressed
like that?
You think you
can compete
with us?
That you're
one of us?
A man
making a pass
at our girls,
playacting
like that?
Who do you
think you are?"

I want to run.
To bowl his
spiky-haired,
muscle-shirted,
tough and manly,
bully body
to the ground.
But
I'm frozen
20 feet away.
Ezra's gaze
tells me to hold off.
He can handle it.
"Ah, Batesian mimicry,"
Ezra says calmly.
Coolly.

"Do you know
what it is?"

"What?"
Bo spits.
Eyes squint.

"I said
Batesian mimicry,
you idiot."

Bo's face looks crazed with
disbelief and rage
at the insult.
But whether it is
curiosity or
cowardliness,
second-guessing
or just toying with prey,
something keeps
his fists at bay.
Ezra gives Bo
a slow up and down
with his eyes.

"It's when a harmless species
changes itself to look
like a harmful species.
They appear to be
more of a threat than
they actually are."

"Harmless?
I'll show you,
freak," Bo says.

"You're
gonna wish
I was harmless."

Bo raises his fist
to strike when
my instinct
kicks in.
I leap
at him.
I knock him
across the side
of the head with
a backpack
full of
books.

He stumbles
backward
to the ground.
Looks up
at me
with
hate
and
surprise.

His friend Derek
rushes over
to help him up.
Ready
to jump into
the fight.

But
Bo
stops
him.

"We're
done here,"
he says,
as he shoots us
a look
that
could
kill.
And
walks
away.

A Memory I Wish Was a Blur

That moment.
It was brief
but
long enough
to send me
spiraling into
a flashback:

It's September of
my freshman year and
my first of
the high school parties
on the other side
of the quarry.

I've had a
few too many
red plastic cups
and didn't feel it
until now.
Until the music from
car radios is pounding
the inside of my skull.
Like water beating
against a boulder.
And the darkening sky is
blurring like everything
is underwater.
Images seem bent.
Sound is wet and slurred.

I lost track
of Renny
an hour or so ago.
When Victoria
showed up
in a leather jacket and
rose-red lipstick.

I stumble toward
the spinning
oaks and maples.
Because
I think
I need
to pee. Or
get some air. Or
not be
slammed with
all this noise.
A branch
snaps
behind
me.

Bo
backs me
against
a broad tree.
His arms
blocking
my escape
on
either
side.

His torso
presses
heavily
against mine.
Pushing me
into the trunk.

His breath
smells rotten
as
his mouth
bites
my
collarbone.

I can't kick or
move my arms or
even speak.
Just a
grumble.
Then suddenly,
a miracle.
It stops.

Strong arms
yank Bo
off me.
Throw him
to the ground.
Strong arms.
The arms of
a baseball star.
Arms of
a carpenter.

Arms of
an older brother.

"If you ever
touch
my sister again,
I will personally
show you why
they say I have
the best swing
in the county.
You
understand?"

Bo coughs
and spits.
Throws up
in the dirt
before nodding.

We leave him
on the
forest floor.
Renny flips
the matted hair
out of his face.
He stretches
my arm around
his shoulder
and takes
me home.

An Understanding

This is why
there is a
comfort
in seeing
a woman's
eyes
gaze back
from
within
a boy's
body.

If he knows
what it is
to be
rough-
handled
for being
too strong
in the
wrong
ways.
For being
not strong
enough
in the
traditional
ways.

If he knows
what it is
to fear
a man.
To both
love
and fear
his own
softness.
To fear
rough
hands.

Then he is
not
to be
feared.

He is
like
me.

A Heartbreak

It's late
on a Sunday night
and I follow
the sobs
to Renny's door.
Dragging
my stool
behind me.

He gives a
half-hearted
nod.
I enter.

Victoria
broke up
with him.
He
discovered
she'd been
cheating
with a
football player
from the
community
college.

I can see
the hurt
and

confusion
on his face.
Though
I knew
something like
this
would happen,
the protective
anger
waterfalls
inside me.

It grows
tentacles.
Until
it is
a sea monster.
Tearing
the
U.S.S.
Victoria
apart.
Board
by
slimy
board.

My anger becomes
a creature
of the deep.
Scaled
and
finned
and
terrible.

I want to
spear her.
Or
swallow
her whole.
Or
drag her down
to an
ocean trench.
Where
she can see
nothing
but darkness.
So her vision
will match
her
stupid
terrible
heart.

A Disagreement

"Well,
things like that
happen,"
Ezra says,
with a shrug.
"It sucks, but
you have to
let people
be people."

I'm taken aback.
"How can
you say that?
She cheated on
my brother."

My brother who
adored her.
Who
was nothing
but
kind
and gentle.
Who
she
didn't
deserve.

Renny.
My brother.

"That sucks,
I know," Ezra says,
"But
people have
different needs.
Changing needs. And
maybe she and
your brother just
didn't have what
they once had."

Then
it happens.
I run
out
of
words.
In fact, I
can't
say
anything.

My face becomes
the top of
a still lake.
Alive with unseen
snapping turtles. Or
a river pool hiding
deadly currents
just below
the surface.

"I have to go,"
I say coldly.

Makeshift Horoscope for Today

Later that day I
find a scrap piece
of paper
tucked inside
my locker.

Pisces:
Today is not a day
to be ruled
by anger.
Forgive
those
around you.

(Especially
cute Capricorns
who
don't like
being
on your
bad side.)

A Proposal

"You know
what would
really put you
on my good side?"
I whisper
in the hallway
into Ezra's ear.

He perks up.
A wicked grin
spreads across
his face.

"What?"

I grab his hands
and hold them
lightly
in mine.

"Come
down
to
the
river
with
me."

April

The scent of
spring rain and
damp earth
fills the gorge.

The leaves
have returned,
green and
youthful.
The water is
crisp and
eager
to race,
free
of ice.

We take
the first drop
head on.
I peek
at Ezra with
sneaky,
smiling eyes.

The spray
messes up his
dark curls.
He shivers and
laughs
nervously.
Too nervously.

I take in his
wide eyes.
The hands
groping for
a grip on
the side of
the boat.
He's
afraid.

I watch him
closely
for the rest
of the trip,
making sure
not to
knock his seat
too hard
on any
rocks.

The other guests
climb out.
Roaring with
laughter.
Wildly
recapping
every bend
and brace.
I ask
what he
thinks
of the river.
My river.

I motion toward
the light rippling
across
the water's surface.
The home the
beaver built
off the bank.
The stillness
pierced by
the sharp cry
of a hawk.

"It's okay,"
he says.

My mouth
drops like
a ledge rapid.

"Just okay?"

"It's not really
my thing.
But thanks
for taking me."

The river
inside me
stops
gushing.

A worry pops up:
what if we're
not the same,
not at all?

A Concern

I pick
chocolate hazelnut,
to Sam's
dismay.

"Why do you
have to ruin
a perfectly good
chocolate milkshake
with nuts?"
he grumbles.

"Because
it's my turn and
you can have it
your way
next week."

It took some
time and
convincing. But
Sam has seemed
to finally
warm up to the idea
of Ezra and me
together. Which is funny,
because
we've been that way
for half a year now.

"He's going
to art school,
Sam.
Three hours away."

"Well, does that mean
you're not
dating anymore?"

"No,
no," I say.
"We'll just
see less
of each other.
But
he says
he'll visit
every other weekend.
And
I can come stay
with him
when I want to."

"Okay," Sam says.
"So
there's
nothing really
to worry about then?"

He looks up from
the milkshake glass,
straw still in mouth.
A slight frown
from the hazelnut.

I look away
and
blow the end
of my
straw wrapper
into
his
freckled face.

"No.
There's
nothing
to worry
about."

Summer Montage

I'm not sure
exactly
what
happiness
is.
But
the summer
passes by
in a string of
beautiful
barefoot
hours.

Stones
are skipped
to the beat of
the music
of a late dusk.

A soft guitar riff
is made from
the twangy
feeling of
grass
between
our toes.

We have
time

to not
overthink
thinking.
Just
admire the
bustling traffic
of forest floors.
Tire swings
dangling from
oak arms.
And the way
his fingers
brush across
my back like
the little green
inchworms
I've been finding
all over.
Every day.

I'm not
exactly sure
what perfect
happiness is.
But this
has got
to be
close.
I say
the
inchworms
will make me

think
of him.

Of the
stinging sweetness
of August,
when we laid
in the grass and
counted
the
remaining
days.

Inchworms.
Small
green
reminders
of
a
beautiful
green
boy.

Full of life.
Full of growth.
Full of earth.
I'm not sure
which is harder:
not knowing
someone you love
is leaving,
or knowing it

and still
holding
him.

He makes
me promise
to care for
the greenhouse.
It's now bursting with
every color in
my vocabulary.

I make him promise
to come back for
my art display.
The coffee shop is
letting me have
it there in the fall.

"I promise," he says.

Quarry, Sturgeon Moon

The night before
Ezra leaves,
we sit
by the quarry.
He plays
me a song
he wrote on
the mandolin.

"It's for you,"
he says.
"A water song."

I close my eyes so
I can really hear it.
Swells and currents
stream through
a loose,
floating melody.
With notes that
plink
like raindrops.
And some that
ebb and flow
like great
sweeping tides.

"I love it," I say.

He looks up
while
still playing.
And says,
"I love you, Hannah."

We curl up like
a wave
on the ground.
Arms wrapped
around
each other's
bodies.
Under a full moon
he
did not pray to
tonight.
But,
then again,
I think
this
is a kind
of
prayer,
too.

After, Day 1

The sky is
an empty shell today.
Color sucked out
like an oyster.
Foggy, like
the remains
of a dream.
Like it will
wake up
any second
now
to take
inventory
of what's
missing.

Ezra took
the colors
with him
when he left.
Which makes sense,
I guess.
They flocked to
the ones inside him.
Drawn to
like company.
Migrating too soon.
Too soon.
Where
did he learn
to do that?

And
when
will they
come back?

After, Day 10

Who was I
before
that did not know
this feeling?
I was whole and
self-contained,
sure.
But
I woke up
every morning
without
trying to remember
the smell of
someone else's skin.

Like
recalling a dream
on the tip
of my tongue.
Or just behind
the eyelids.
Without the fingers'
hazy memory
of curls sprung.
Arms touched.

Who was I
before that did not know
this feeling?

After, Day 30

It's been
a month.

He stopped
writing
me letters.

He hasn't
returned
my phone call
for
a week
now.

We're in
a drought
and I
haven't seen
a
single
inchworm
since
he
left.

An Unwelcome Truth

Sam doesn't look himself tonight.
Like he has a sour taste in his mouth
that seems to have nothing to do with
the coconut lime milkshake I forced on him.

"Okay, just tell me whatever it is
that's been bothering you for the last hour.
I'll buy you a Reese's shake," I say.

Sam shifts in the booth,
like he's weighing a great problem.
I take our fries hostage
until he gives in.
"I think I saw Ezra tonight," he says.
Not meeting my eyes.

"What? Where?"

"On the far corner of Main Street.
By the theater.
I'm not positive because
he changed direction when I saw him.
Started toward the quarry path."

"That's not possible," I stammer.

He's still not meeting my gaze.
I can tell there's something else

he's not telling me.
"Sam, I…"

"He was with someone else, Hannah.
A girl I didn't recognize."

That's when confusion
and hurt turn into rage.
A rage that seems to be
the only alternative to silence.

"You're wrong," I practically shout.
Turning a few heads nearby.
"You've just always been waiting
for him to mess up somehow.
You see a guy who looks
a little like him from far away
and think the worst."

Now it's my turn
to leave the booth early.
The milkshake unfinished.
The friend sitting alone.
I storm outside.

I need the comfort of the river.
But a voice somewhere
in the back of my head,
in the folds of my heart,
in the pit of my stomach, says,
Don't go to the quarry tonight.
There's no comfort for you there.

Troubling Phone Conversation #1

"Hannah,
it's not that
I don't want
to see you.
I do.
I'm just
figuring
some things out
right now.
And
it has
to happen
here.
Not in
that town."

That town.
It's the
first time
since he
moved here
that he's made it
so apparent
he's an outsider.
That he
doesn't belong.
"Things?
What things?

I'll help you
figure them out."

"No.
Thank you,
but no," he says.
"It has to
be just
me.

It's just,
I'm
a different
person
here and
I don't
know
who to be
when
I go
back to
a place I
already
left
behind."

Left behind.
Ouch.

Troubling Phone Conversation #2

"Hannah,
I didn't cheat
on you.
Nothing happened. But
I've been
learning
about this
thing where
someone is
in more
than one
relationship
at a time.
And I think
I need
to try it."

"We
need to
try it?" I ask.

"We.
Yeeeessss.
We."

You hesitated,
I want to say.

"It's just,
people have
different needs.
Changing needs,
and…"

*Where have I
heard this before?*

Immediately,
I remember
my brother
wiping
puffy,
red eyes.
Hiding them
beneath
his old
baseball cap
while I sat
on my stool.
My head
on his shoulder.
My arm around
his back.

"And we just
don't have
what we
once had?"
I ask.

"What?
No.
It's not
like that.
It's hard to
explain.
I still love you.
It's just that
this is
something
separate.

It's kind of
like,
so
you know how
I'm a
Capricorn?
Earth,
right?
Well,
I still have
a lot of
Sagittarius.
Fire.
And sometimes
I need to
let that take
a little
more
control."

"And burn
everything
you planted?"
I ask.

"Well,
I mean,
sometimes
scorch and burn is
a healthy way to
clear the landscape.
Let the fire
take over
for a bit
so that the earth
can grow better
afterwards.

Being with
other people,
it wouldn't mean
anything.
Just something new.
Wouldn't change
how I feel
about you.
It's just not
all that
fair
to expect
monogamy.
Just one person

for each person."

I bite my lip
and command
the water inside me
not to slip out
of my eyes.

"Maybe you
should just
leave your landscape
unplanted
for a
while.
That does
the same
trick,"
I say.

"Don't
be
like
that,"
he says.

Unanswered Voicemail
from Ezra #1

"Listen,
I'm sorry.
I can tell
this
hurts
you.

We don't have
to do this
if you
don't want to.

Just promise me
you'll think
it over
and
get back
to me.

I'll come home
next weekend and
you can show me
all the amazing things
you've been making
for that art show
of yours."

Quarry, Harvest Moon

There's a full moon tonight.
The first since
he's been gone.
Which means he's
burning
a bundle of sage.
Prayers wafting
upward
like smoke.

It's the same moon
hearing his pleas
tonight
that is
also there
for me.
Over 100
miles away.
And I wonder
if he ever said
a prayer
for that.
I wonder
if he ever said
a prayer
for me.
The moon says
she owes

me
nothing.
That this
is how
it should
be.

The boy who
used to
sit with me
under the moon
says
he owes
me
nothing.

I don't
believe this
is how
it should
be. But,
even when
he's gone,
the moon
tells me
to love
him just
the same.
I remember
his words.
"You have to
let people

be people."

I've always
wanted him
to be
himself.
I love him
for always
being
himself.
But
I've been
trying
to stomach
the idea of
him holding
someone else.
And
it comes
to this:
There are just
some things
I'm
not okay
with us
being.

A Knowing

Renny
senses
we
need
to
talk
before
I've
even
made
it
to
his
door
with
the
stool.

"It's
about
Ezra,
isn't
it?"

I let go
of everything.

The secret visit.
The unanswered
messages.
The college girls
taking
my place.

When I finish,
his face
is a mix of
stumped
and
concerned.

He doesn't threaten
to go beat up
my boyfriend.
Or get angry like
a lot of brothers
would. And
I've always loved him
for that.
He's protective,
but
he realizes that
most of the time,
I need to protect
myself.
"Relationships
are hard,
complicated
things,

Hannah.
It sounds
like
you're
starting off
with
a tough one."

He gives
a slight smile.
Then
he
adjusts
his
baseball
cap
and
leans
forward.

Real
talk.

"So,
I've always found
it's best not
to change
for people.
Much better
to change
because
of people.

A relationship
can teach you
things you
carry on
to
your next one.
It can
change your
perspective or
what you find
you want.
But,
if someone
asks you
to change
for them
in a way
you really can't,
then sometimes
you just can't."

A Decision

I pick up
the phone and
finally
call Ezra back.

"I can't do
what you want.
I thought about it.
If I
pretended like
it was okay
with me,
I just know
it would
eat me up inside.
Until I became
a mimosa
or
poison ivy.
And then
I wouldn't
be
me
and
we wouldn't
be
us.

You would
lose me.
That's what
would happen."

A Response

I expected
that
to be
the end
of the
conversation.

He said we
didn't have
to do it
if
I didn't
want to.
That it
mattered
to him
if
it hurt
me.
But
he
sounded
frustrated.

"You just
don't understand.
You can't
expect me

to just be
the old me
when
I've been
changing
here.
And
I could be
this new me
with
girls here.
And we
would
still have
what we
had before.
I'd
probably
come
home
less,
but…"

"You don't
come home
now," I say.

"Because it
makes me anxious.
I don't know who
to be right now."

"You always
seemed
to me
like you
know exactly
who you are.

That's one of
the things I
like
best
about
you," I say.

Ezra sighs.
"I still love you
and I
want to be
in a relationship
with you.
So I
won't have
a relationship
here then.
Okay?
Happy?
I'll just stick to
a few
meaningless
romances
on the side.

Nothing
emotional.
Just
figuring out
attraction and
desire and
myself.
Okay?"

I know.
I know,
it's
not
the same.
At all.
But
I can't help
the
flashback.
That
flashback.

The drunken
quarry night
and
all that
emotionless
touching.

If that is
really what
he wants,

then
maybe
we're not
as alike
as
I thought.

A Resolution

"No.
Not okay.
I love
you,
but
I love
myself,
too,"
I say.
"You might
not know
who you
are yet,
but
I know me.
And if you
don't want
me,
then I
don't want
this.
The day you
touch someone else
is the day
we're
through.
Decide."

A long pause
and
a deep sigh.
"Okay,
okay.
I'll drop it."

A Completion

A few days later,
I put the finishing touches
on the paintings of
Ezra and me.

One of us
floating on our backs
through
a star-speckled sky.

Another of him
playing
mandolin
on top of
the moon.
Colors gushing
from
the neck of
the instrument.

At least
half a dozen
more.
Finally ready
to show him.

Unanswered Voicemail #2

He left me
a message saying
he has a test
on Monday.
He can't
come home
after all.

An anchor
digs into
my chest.

Fine.
I trade Renny
my best
flannel shirt
for a day
with
his truck.
Renny takes
the shirt and
I head off
to surprise
my
flaky
art student
of a
boyfriend.

Surprise Visit, October

The campus is
so much bigger
and fancier
than I ever thought.

Marble pillars and
cobbled paths.
Definitely not out of
an old dairy
and lumber town.

The women here wear
heels and leather jackets.
Makeup that
makes them look French
and cat-like.

I have no idea
which dorm is his.
I'm counting on him
being in the library,
cramming. But,
as I cross the courtyard,
I hear, "Hannah?"

I turn. And say,
"Victoria?"

In the flesh.

She wears
a bright red
miniskirt and
a sheer midriff shirt.
A kerchief
tied around her neck
to complete
the outfit.

Blonde hair
puffs out
to her shoulders
as she stretches
her long
model legs
beside a man-made
pond.

I'm planning on
just giving her
a grade-A
stink eye and
walking by.
Then I do
a double-take.
There's a boy sitting
so close to her.
Too close.
He's wearing
a button-up

black shirt
with the V
opened up
on his chest.
Neatly trimmed
Beard.
Close-cropped
haircut on the sides
with
the top longer
and slicked back.
But
those eyes.
Those
bright green
eyes and a
stray dark curl
poking out on
his temple.

"Ezra?"

A Betrayal

Now I'm
walking fast.
Straight
toward them.
I can't
help it.

Ezra jumps up
in surprise.
Victoria just
looks me
up and down
in my
oversized
sweater,
loose
jeans,
and
ratty
beanie.
And
laughs.

"You look
just like
your brother,"
she snickers.

"So
what's
wrong
with
that,
princess?"
I shoot back.
I look
to Ezra for
some form
of support.

Now it's
my turn
to be
surprised.
Ezra looks
nervous
and
embarrassed.

"Jeez,
Hannah,"
he says,
under his breath.
"Do you have to be
such a *boy*
sometimes?"

Before running,
wordless,
to Renny's

truck,
I throw
my whole
stack
of paintings
right
into
the
pond.

I hope all
the colors
run together.
And
the pictures
all blur
beyond
recognition.
Like
his memories.
Like
how I
must have
always been
in his
memory.

Quarry, New Moon

I skipped
Coffee Shop
Friday.

That night
the drought
breaks.
Everything
the sky
has been
holding back
thrashes
and
floods.
Rain
beating
down
on the land
as I sit,
sopping wet
and
not
caring
at
all.
It feels
good
to see

the water
wailing
and
commanding
the earth
like
the sorceress
it always
was.

That's right,
I think
to myself.
Water is
the
strongest
force
on
earth.
I am
more
powerful.
And
I will
erode
him.

I realize
all the women
I know
are rivers.
Peaceful.

Beautiful.
Able to
calm
a man
with one
look.

Fierce.
Stormy.
Able to
destroy
a man
in one
blow.

Men have tried
to navigate them.
Use them for
their own purposes.
But, when it
comes down to it,
the rivers are
the true force
to be
reckoned with.
Men gain
safe passage
by learning
to respect
a river.

Because
the river
gives
and takes
as it chooses.

And,
after all
these years,
I've decided
the river
is
a woman.

Yes.
She must be
a woman.
To allow
so many
men
in her waters
and still be
as strong
as she
is.

An Uprooting

There is still dirt
under my fingernails
from ripping up
half the plants in
his greenhouse.

The ginkgos
because
I don't want
to remember.

The jasmines
because
we're not
in love.

The clovers
because
I don't want
to think of him.

There is still dirt
under my fingernails
from him.
There is still *him*
under my fingernails.

An Offering

The night
quickly
grows cold
and dark.
But
I can't
move.
Can't
leave.
So I
lie down
and fall
asleep.

I awake to
a wool blanket
draped across
my body.
Logs
crackling.
The smell of
smoke and
a pile of wood
stacked neatly
behind me.
A reflector fire.

Laying in
the dirt,
next to the
makeshift pit.
Glowing
in the
orange light
is
a
purple
lighter.

Voicemails I Don't Leave #1

I know
in the beginning
you wanted
more of
a label.
A banner.
A cry to rally
behind.

I didn't know
how to do that.

This was
the best I had.
The woman
in me
loved the man
in you.
Loved the boy
in you.
Loved the woman
in you.
Loved the woman,
the boy woman
in me.
The boy
in me
loved the woman

in you.
The woman
in me
loved the woman
in you.
In you, in you,
in you.
The lines blur,
but
I know I loved
in you.
I didn't know what
to call that.
Or me.
Or us.

I didn't know I had
to call it anything
in particular.
That,
like a dog,
it would
only answer to
a specific name.
I never wanted
to collar it
anyways.
The woman
in the boy
in the woman in me
loved the woman
in the boy

in the woman in you.
But
I do know that,
in the end,
it was
the man
in you
that left
the woman
in me.
Yes.
In the end,
it was
the man.

And that,
in particular.
In naming.
In calling
it out for
what it is.
Is what
is so
hard to
forgive.

Voicemails I Don't Leave #2

Horoscope for tomorrow:

Time is in
the house of
your head.
Your heart is of
its own rising.
Do not forget
the stars
from which
you come.
But
make
your
own
darn
future.

Voicemails I Don't Leave #3

And in the end,
it comes to this.
People are at once
endlessly
more complicated
and
remarkably
more simple
than
I
ever
thought.

November

The night of my
art show arrives.
And no one has seen
my new paintings.
I holed myself up
in my room for
the last month
to make them
after drowning
my entire exhibition
in the pond at
Ezra's school.

I'm wearing a
billowy blue dress,
a plaid shirt,
my usual Converse sneakers,
and a nervous smile.

One by one,
the town piles in.
Teachers.
Classmates.
My river rafting boss.
Renny.
Sam.
They circle the room
without speaking.

Take in
my portraits.
Portraits of my
water dreams.

A painting of
a single flame
lit inside
a waterfall.
Portrait of
longing.

A painting of
waves crashing
through the open doors
of a half-ruined barn.
Portrait of
misplacement.

A painting of
a violinist
fiddling underwater in
a hidden bog.
Portrait of
fantasy.

And so on.

A Recognition

The coffee shop
eventually empties.
Sam and I
sit down
to split
a chocolate banana
milkshake.

He's still looking up
at the paintings
in the kind
of trance
I first found
him in
all those
years ago.

Then,
he turns to me
and says,
"Your titles
feel right.
But
they're also
missing something
important."

"And what's that?"

I ask,
shooting my
straw wrapper
at his chest.

"They're
self-portraits,
too."

January

I've been
talking
to Renny
lately
about college
next year.
About
going away
to school
on the
other side
of the
country.

Leaving is
a scary thought.
But
never leaving
scares me, too.
I want to be
in an
outdoor program
where I can
learn to guide
bigger water.

Plus I've
never lived
by the ocean.

And,
well.
Like all water,
I kind of
always knew
I'd find myself
ending up there.

I'll come home
to visit
as much
as I can.

I've already
promised Sam
I'd write
every week.

He's staying
in town
to learn
welding.
He's
all excited
about getting to
play with
fire
for a living.

A Brother's Advice

Last night
I brought
the stool in.
Talked
the idea
over with
my brother.
I told him
I was
scared.

"What
if
I
can't
do
it?"

He adjusted
his ball cap
and leaned
forward.

"You know,
Hannah.
Someday
someone
is going to

tell you
you can't
do something.
And then
you'll go
and do it.
It'll be
a great
feeling.
But
it'll make
you wonder
all the things
you didn't
do before
because someone told you
you couldn't
and you
could
have.

I believe
in you,"
he added.

Wind

Renny,
I've decided,
is air.
Wind.

He's the breath
you need when
everything else
feels like
too much.

He's the gentle push
in the right direction.
The nudge forward
to help you along.

Wind and water
together
make for either
a smooth day
of sailing or
a perfect storm.

Not
a bad
team.

Quarry, Crow Moon

The moon
is full
tonight.
For the
first time,
I burn
a bundle
of
sage.

I pray
for Renny.
For Sam.
For my
last months
of school
and for
the big
trip
west.

Then,
I
pray
for
Ezra.
I pray
that someday

he'll learn
to love
a river.
To respect
the water.
Because then,
maybe,
he'll know
how
to
treat
a
woman.

Water Dream #4

Somehow I know
it is 10 years
or so
in the future.

I'm not sure how.
Because
we look older,
sure. But
mostly the same.

Ezra has
patches of dust
on his body,
like a quilt of
garden plots.
One from
every place
he's been since
I last saw him.

I am wearing
a cloak of raindrops.
One from
every bit of sky
I've thirsted under.
We look
each other

up and down
slowly.
Carefully.
Saying nothing
and everything
all at once.

His eyes are
soft.
Apologetic.
Understanding.

Mine are
steady but
kind.
Forgiving.

I am water
and
he is earth.
But
somewhere
in between
that look
is
a meeting
of the
two.
In this place,
there's a
shoreline
we both

can accept.
Before
turning
and
walking
our
separate
ways.

WANT TO KEEP READING?

If you liked this book, check out another book
from West 44 Books:

MANNING UP
BY BEE WALSH

ISBN: 9781538382677

EYES ON THE PRIZE

Today at practice,
Coach asks me
where I see myself
in five years.

Five years.

   "Here, I guess."

   "No son,
   where do you want
   to be?"

   "Here, I guess."

   "Jack,
   you need to get
   your eyes on the prize."

The prize.

What is
the prize?

ANYTHING

I'd give anything
to be able
to put on
invisible clothes
like that wizard kid
in that book.

Walk around
and no one
would look
at me.

No one
would pat me
on the shoulder

and ask me
about the game.

No one
would ask me
how my mother

is holding up.

I could do
anything
and no one
would say anything
about it.

Check out more books at:
www.west44books.com

An imprint of Enslow Publishing

WEST **44** BOOKS™

About the Author

Meg Specksgoor is a poet and river-rafting guide from Western New York, currently living in northern New Mexico. She graduated from Houghton College with a Bachelor of the Arts in English and writing with minors in art and intercultural studies. She likes campfires, breakfast, adventuring, and people who tell her interesting stories in combination with any of those activities.